The Berenstain Bears®

BEDTIME STORY

Stan & Jan Berenstain

GT
PUBLISHING

Outside the Bears' tree house, there was much stretching and yawning and settling down.

Mother Nightingale was singing a soft lullaby to her hatchlings.

Mother and Father Squirrel were cuddling their young.

And Mrs. Bunny was making
a final count of her sleeping babies.

Even the sun had all but settled down
just beyond the horizon.

But *inside* the tree house, lights were ablaze, the television was aglow, and playthings carpeted the carpet. The scene was set: the bedtime battle was about to begin.

"Time for bed!" said Mama Bear. "Time to turn off the TV and start picking up your things!"

"Can't we stay up just a little longer?" said Sister Bear. "Just a wee bit longer! Please!"

"Can't we even watch the *beginning* of the next show?" asked Brother Bear.

"Not even the first commercial!" said Mama as she turned off the television.

"Wha? Byrsk! Huh?" sputtered Papa Bear, who had fallen asleep during the evening news. Good for Papa. Now he would be well-rested for the battle ahead.

"Most of the things on the floor are Brother's!"
said Sister.
"No, they're not!" said Brother.

Mama held up the piece of embroidery she had
been working on. "Read this, please," she said.

FATHER, MOTHER,
SISTER, BROTHER,
WE PITCH IN AND
HELP EACH OTHER.

Pretty soon, everything was
picked up and put away.

"Piggyback! Piggyback!" shouted Sister as Papa headed up the stairs.
"Me too! Me too!" shouted Brother as Sister climbed on Papa's back.

Mama climbed the stairs behind them.
Papa needed a little push at the top.

Papa went into the bathroom to get things ready for the cubs' bath.

"Let's see, now," he said. "Bubble bath, back brush, cub shampoo..."

"And TUB TOYS!" shouted the cubs as they dumped armloads of toys into the tub. There were so many toys that there wasn't any room for the water.

"Only two tub toys per customer," said Papa.
As Brother and Sister chose their tub toys, Papa measured out the bubble bath.

Within minutes the bathroom was filled with bubbles and Papa was shouting, "Stop the bubbles!" Mama came a-running.

"How much bubble bath did you put in?" she asked.

"A cupful, just as it says on the bottle," said Papa.

"It doesn't say a cupful," said Mama. "It says a *capful*!"

"Oh," said Papa. He was starting to look like he needed another nap.

"Ish-isha-way we rush our teeth! Rush our teeth! Rush our teeth!" sang the cubs as they brushed their teeth. Soon the cubs were sparkling clean.

But the bathroom wasn't sparkling clean. The bathroom was a wet, soggy mess.

"I'll get the cubs into their pajamas and start them on their prayers while you straighten up the bathroom," said Mama.

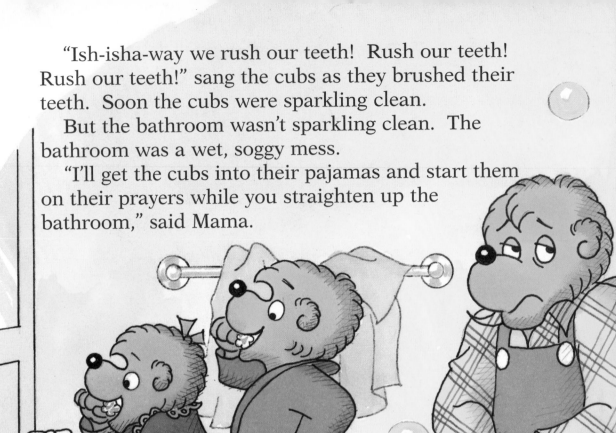

Now Papa was really
starting to look like
he needed another nap.

By the time Papa finished his cleanup chore, the cubs were well into their prayers.

"Those'll be quite enough blessings, thank you," said Mama. "It's time for you to choose your bedtime stories."

BLESS FARMER AND MRS. BEN AND THEIR HORSE, BLESS OUR TEDDIES, BLESS OUR PUPPY- LITTLE LADY, BLESS FROGGY PUPPET, BLESS HONEY BUNNY...

Brother chose *The Three Billy Goats Gruff.*
Sister chose *Goldibear and the Three People.*

Papa managed to get as far as the
second Billy Goat Gruff's crossing the
bridge before he fell sound asleep.

Mama finished both stories.

She tucked the cubs in and put a blanket on Papa. Then she turned off the top light,

switched on the night-light, kissed them all good night,

and tiptoed out of the room.